Raccoon at Clear Creek Road

SMITHSONIAN'S BACKYARD

For Ross
        — C.O.

For R., S., and Z.
        — C.T.

Book Design: Shields & Partners, Westport, CT

10 9 8 7 6
Printed in China

Acknowledgements:
   Our very special thanks to Dr. Charles Handley of the Department of Vertebrate Zoology
at the Smithsonian's National Museum of Natural History for his curatorial review.

Library of Congress Cataloging-in-Publication Data

Otto, Carolyn.

Raccoon at Clear Creek Road / by Carolyn B. Otto; illustrated by Cathy Trachok.
        p.   cm.
Summary: After leaving her newborn kits to search for food, a mother raccoon is separated
from them by a flooding creek.
        ISBN 1-56899-175-4
1. Raccoons — Juvenile fiction. [1. Raccoons — Fiction.]
I. Trachok, Cathy, ill. II. Title.
        PZ10.3.O848Rac 1995   95-6775
        [E] — dc20   CIP
                                                                        AC

Raccoon at Clear Creek Road

by Carolyn B. Otto

Illustrated by Cathy Trachok

Soundprints™
Where Children Discover...

As a spring afternoon cools into evening, a flock of
starlings settles in a willow behind the yellow house
on Clear Creek Road. Inside the tree, deep within a hollow,
a mother raccoon awakens.

Raccoon listens to the starlings above and the rushing creek
below. She nuzzles her kits, born two days before. Their eyes
are closed and ears shut, but their mouths are open wide. Their
hungry cries sound like the twittering birds.

Raccoon nurses her kits until they grow drowsy with milk. She croons to them. She washes each kit with her tongue.
Once they are clean and fed and fast asleep, Raccoon must find her own dinner. She has not eaten since the kits were born. She climbs from the hollow in the tree, headfirst to the ground.

Light from the windows of the house makes a pattern on the grass. Raccoon moves along in the shadows. She sees well in the night, and darkness hides and protects her.

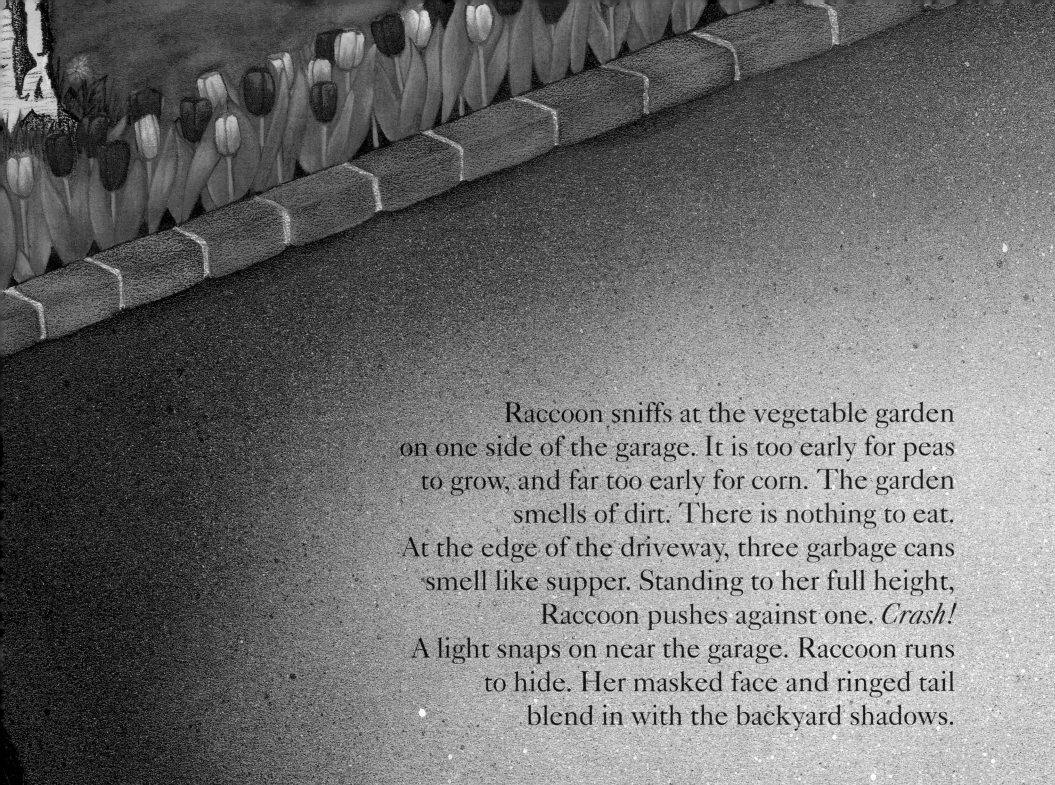

Raccoon sniffs at the vegetable garden
on one side of the garage. It is too early for peas
to grow, and far too early for corn. The garden
smells of dirt. There is nothing to eat.
At the edge of the driveway, three garbage cans
smell like supper. Standing to her full height,
Raccoon pushes against one. *Crash!*
A light snaps on near the garage. Raccoon runs
to hide. Her masked face and ringed tail
blend in with the backyard shadows.

Raccoon hears footsteps, a scraping, a clatter, and the rumble of the garage door moving up and then down. The light goes out. The night is quiet. Raccoon sneaks along the driveway. The garbage cans are gone. The smell of things to eat comes now from the garage. The door is closed. She can not get in.

Hungrier still and thirsty too, Raccoon turns back
toward the creek. A faint twittering overhead makes her
climb the willow. Her kits are sleeping. The sound must
have come from a starling.

Raccoon climbs down again and this time heads for
the water. She stops to drink, then splashes in up to her
belly. With her front paws she explores the shallows.

She touches mud, sticks and a pinecone.
The water feels cold and is running fast with
rain from recent storms. Raccoon wades deeper
to chase the silver flash of a minnow. The pull
of the creek grows stronger. She loses her
footing, and the water sweeps her away.

Raccoon tumbles over drowned branches and a rock.
She goes under. Water rushes above her head, but she struggles
up to the surface. With her nose high, Raccoon paddles to the
other side of the creek. She scrambles up the bank.

She is not hurt, though she is still very
hungry. Raccoon shakes the water from her
fur and cleans off the mud with her tongue.
Raccoon can see her willow tree across
the creek. Light from the yellow house
shines through its branches, and
reflects off a bright piece of tinfoil
near her feet.

27

Raccoon turns the foil over in her paws.
Hidden just beneath it is an earthworm. Food!
She drops the foil to pounce.

Raccoon eats the worm, another worm, and a beetle.
She finds a store of acorns and dried berries, forgotten by
a squirrel. Raccoon eats and eats and feels better.

Hoohoohoo! Raccoon sits up to listen. *Hoohoohoo!* A dark shape sweeps over the water toward the willow.

Her kits could be in danger! Raccoon paces along the bank, looking for a crossing. From a jutting boulder, she leaps to the slick back of a log. She slips and catches herself. Teetering, sliding, she claws her way to the other side of the creek.

Raccoon is at the foot of her tree when she scents a mouse. The smell is strong, delicious, and easy to follow. Raccoon hesitates, sniffing.

Hoohoohoo! The owl wheels
overhead. Raccoon clambers up the
tree. She must protect her kits.
With a rush of nearly silent wings, the
owl dives toward the hollow! Raccoon hisses.
She is ready to fight! But the owl
plummets past her, then plucks
up the mouse and is gone.

Breathing fast, her hair still on end, Raccoon trills to her kits. They are safe and soundly asleep, and they are too young to answer.

Sometime soon their ears will open. And their eyes will open, black and bright. Before long they will be big enough to follow her to the shadowed yard below.

Then the kits will prowl with her around the yellow house on Clear Creek Road. There will be sugar peas in the garden, and sweet corn later on. The creek will grow lazy and slow with the heat of summer. And Raccoon will teach her kits to swim and to fish for silver minnows.

Raccoon snuggles down with her kits, and they begin to twitter.

About the Raccoon

Raccoons are found across America, except in deserts and high mountains. After the sun goes down, raccoons start to look for food. With excellent night vision, they are able to find many kinds of plants and animals to eat. They sometimes swish their food through water as if they are washing it, but they are also kneading it with their sensitive paws. Raccoons have nimble fingers and they like to feel objects, especially things that shine.

Mother raccoons often make nests high up in hollow trees and give birth in the early spring. When the babies are born, they are helpless and small, only three or four inches long. At first, the mother raccoon forages close to the nest. As spring turns into summer, her searches for food gradually lengthen, until the kits have grown enough to come along. By autumn the kits are almost as big as their mother, fat and ready for the winter. The mother raccoon and her young sleep through the long cold months, waking once in a while to forage. When spring comes they separate to begin new raccoon families.

Glossary

croon, trill, twitter: Some of the sounds raccoons make to communicate.

hollow: A cavity formed by rot in a limb or the trunk of a tree.

kit: A baby raccoon, sometimes called a cub or pup.

mask: The dark hair around a raccoon's eyes. The mask may absorb available light, which may help the raccoon see better at night.

starlings: Iridescent black birds that roam in flocks and often damage crops. They were introduced into North America from Europe about a hundred years ago.

tail rings: Alternating light and dark colored bands that encircle a raccoon's tail. A mother's tail rings may be a signal for her kits to follow.

Points of Interest in this Book